LADYBIRD BOOKS, INC.
Auburn, Maine 04210 U.S.A.
© LADYBIRD BOOKS LTD 1992
Loughborough, Leicestershire, England

Printed in U.S.A.

A Balloon
for Katie Kitten

By Joan Stimson
Illustrated by Cathy Beylon

Ladybird Books

Katie Kitten loved balloons. When she saw the balloon man in the park, she squealed with excitement.

"Please, Mom," she begged, "please buy me a balloon."

But Mom wasn't sure. "Those balloons are filled with a gas called helium," she told Katie. "You have to hold on to them very tightly. If you let go, they just float away. Do you think you're grown up enough for a helium balloon?"

"I *am* grown up enough," said Katie. "Can I have one, please? Can I have *that* one?" She pointed to a panda balloon.

Mom sighed and got out her purse. The balloon man beamed and unwound Panda's string. He wanted to wrap the string around Katie's wrist, but Katie couldn't wait. She ran round and round the park with Panda, whooping and shouting.

"Hold tight, Katie Kitten," warned Mom.

But... *whoosh!* Mom's warning was too late. Panda had already floated up into a tree.

Katie didn't like heights, but she climbed the tree bravely and rescued Panda. Mom waited anxiously below.

"I didn't think you were grown up enough," said Mom, when Katie was safely on the ground again. "Now, let me hold Panda. We have shopping to do."

When they got to the department store, Katie grabbed Panda's string and jumped onto the escalator. As they rode upstairs, they had a wonderful view of all the things for sale on each floor.

"Wow, look at those toys!" cried Katie. She pointed to a row of dinosaurs, and...*whoosh!* Off went Panda again.

Panda flew past the toys. He flew past the lamps. He flew past the pots and pans, and came to rest right at the top of the store.

At last Mom and Katie got to the top, too.

"I didn't think you were grown up enough…" began Mom.

"*There's* Panda," cried Katie. "He's sitting on one of the hats!"

The store manager looked very stern. But Katie boldly walked up to him and asked, very politely, if he would get her balloon.

They were just in time. A woman was pointing to the display and asking if she could try on "the cute hat with the panda on top"!

Katie held Panda very tightly while Mom did her shopping.

She hung on hard while they waited for the bus.

And when they walked up Katie's street, she decided to wrap the string around her wrist.

"Panda can live in my room," she said.

Suddenly baby Billy from next door ran over to greet them.
Billy laughed and pointed at Panda. But then he tripped and
bumped his nose!

Katie ran to pick him up. "Don't cry, Billy," she said, and
gave him a hug.

WHOOSH!

"Oh, no!" cried Katie. Panda was floating far, far away.
And this time there was nothing to stop him!

As soon as Billy stopped crying, Katie ran inside and shut herself in her room. She wouldn't come downstairs for supper. She didn't want to read or draw or play dominoes.

Ding-dong! went the doorbell. When Katie heard it, she hid her head under her pillow.

After a while, Mom called upstairs, "Katie, there's a visitor for you."

But Katie called back, "I'm not... grown up enough... for visitors!"

"Nonsense!" boomed a friendly voice. It was Grandpa Purrpurr. Mom had told him all about their adventures.

"If you're grown up enough to climb a tree without getting hurt," said Grandpa, "and to speak politely to a store manager, and to comfort baby Billy—then you're grown up enough for me!"

Katie thought about what Grandpa said. She began to feel a little better. At last she came downstairs.

"Hold tight, Katie Kitten," said Grandpa. He opened his arms wide to scoop Katie up. But he let go of the balloon he had brought her!

Whoosh! Elephant floated all the way upstairs, right into Katie's room.

Grandpa, Mom, and Katie looked at each other and laughed.

"Oh, Grandpa," cried Katie, "I don't think you're grown up enough for a helium balloon!"